panda series

**PANDA books are for first readers
beginning to make their own way
through books.**

For Elaine and Colin, with love

Can YOU spot the panda
hidden in the story?

Danny was not happy.
His little sister Susie
was getting birthday presents.

'She's only one!'
he muttered.
'What good is **one**?'

Granny smiled at Susie.
'Happy birthday, dear!'
She gave Susie
a big, sloppy kiss.
'Now, open your present, dear!'
she said.

Danny watched as Susie
tore the paper off.
'Dolly!' said Susie.

'This is a very special dolly!'
said Granny.
'This is **BABY DO IT ALL**!'

Danny didn't like
BABY DO IT ALL.
She looked silly.
Her legs were bent and fat
and she had no hair.
Just a big, plastic head.

Granny bounced the doll
on her knee.

'Hee! Hee! Hee!'
said **BABY DO IT ALL**.

Then Granny put the doll
lying down.

'Waa! Waa! Waa!'
cried **BABY DO IT ALL**.

Granny got the doll's bottle
and filled it with water.

She fed **BABY DO IT ALL**.
Soon the bottle was empty.

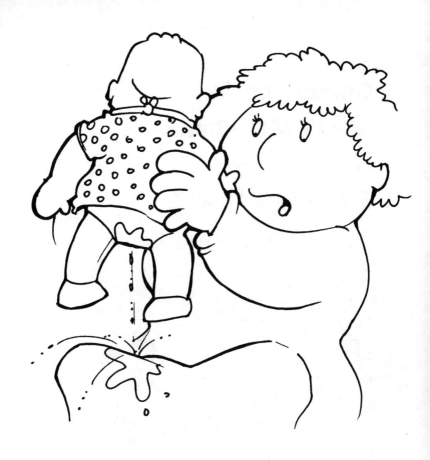

Granny squeezed
the doll's tummy.
Some drops of water fell
on Granny's dress.

Granny smiled.
'**BABY DO IT ALL**
can laugh and
BABY DO IT ALL
can cry,' said Granny.

'But best of all,
BABY DO IT ALL can **wet**!'

Everyone thought
BABY DO IT ALL
was wonderful.
Everyone except Danny.

'She laughs, she cries
and she wets!' he said.
'So what!
Even Susie can do that!'

Mum gave Danny a cross look.
'Go and play,' she said.

Danny ran off to get
his toy gun.
'Guns are better than dolls,'
he said.

Danny's gun was terrific.
He had paper caps for it.
When Danny put the caps in,
the gun made a real bang.
You could even
smell the smoke.

Danny ran back into
the sitting room.
'Baddies beware!' he yelled.

He pulled the trigger.
Bang! Bang! went the gun.

Granny nearly fell off
her chair.
'Good heavens!'
she cried.
'What's that?'

'It's my gun!' said Danny.

'The caps make a great bang.
Isn't it cool, Granny?'

Danny took all the caps
from his pockets
to show them to Granny.
He put them on the table
beside her.

Mum was getting some
tea ready.

'Be careful, Danny,' she said.
'If those caps get wet,
they won't work anymore.'

But Danny wasn't listening.
'Guns are better than dolls,
aren't they, Granny?'
said Danny.
He made a face at Susie.

Susie didn't mind.

She was having fun with

BABY DO IT ALL.

She made the doll laugh.

She made the doll cry.

She gave the doll a bottle.

Then Susie held her doll
over the table.
'**Dolly wee wee**!' she said.

'**No**!' cried Danny.
'Not on my caps!'

But it was too late.
BABY DO IT ALL
had done it!

Danny's caps were
soaking wet.

Danny was very cross.
He punched **BABY DO IT ALL**.
'I'll get you for this!'
he yelled.

'Hee! Hee! Hee!'
laughed **BABY DO IT ALL**.

Later that night,
Danny crept into Susie's room.
He could hear Susie's snores.

That doll must be here
somewhere,
thought Danny.
And I'm going to break it!

Danny bent over the cot.

BABY DO IT ALL

was lying beside Susie.
Danny lifted the doll out.
Susie moved her head.
But she didn't open her eyes.

'Got you, Baldy,'
whispered Danny.

'Danny!' called Dad suddenly.
'What are you doing
in Susie's room?'

Danny hugged the doll.
'I was just saying goodnight
to **BABY DO IT ALL**!'
he whispered.

Danny put the doll back
in Susie's cot.
'I'll get you later!'
he hissed.

Next morning,
Susie sat in her high chair.
She was playing with
BABY DO IT ALL.

Suddenly,
BABY DO IT ALL fell.
Cornflakes splashed
all over Susie.

Mum threw the doll
to Danny.
'Hold this,' she said.
'I must clean Susie.'

Danny was delighted.

He made a fierce face at

BABY DO IT ALL.

'Got you!' he growled.

Danny raced upstairs.

'There must be a battery
in this doll,' he said.
'I'll take it out.
Then **BABY DO IT ALL**
won't do very much!'

But Danny couldn't find
a battery anywhere.
He shook **BABY DO IT ALL**.
'Hee! Hee! Hee!'
said **BABY DO IT ALL**.

'The noise is coming
from the head!'
cried Danny.
'The battery must be in there.
'I'll just take the head off!'

Danny pulled and pulled
at the doll's head.
But **BABY DO IT ALL**'s head
wouldn't come off.

He twisted it
and turned it.
But **BABY DO IT ALL**
was very well made.

Danny had a great idea.
He got his box of
plastic tools from the cupboard.

Then Dad shouted to Danny.
'Time for school!' he called.

Danny grabbed his schoolbag.
He stuffed **BABY DO IT ALL**
into the bag.
He threw in all his tools.
'I'll sort out this doll at school!'
he said.

At school Danny held
his bag tightly.

'What have you got
in there?' asked Mark.
'It's a **secret**!' said Danny.

Someone pushed Danny.
It was Conor Daly.
'What's your secret, Danny?'
he yelled.

Danny held his bag
even more tightly.
'Buzz off, Conor Daly!'
he said.

'Teacher!' shouted Conor Daly.
'Danny has something
for our display table.'

Miss Wise was very pleased.

'Well done, Danny,' she said.
'Let's see what it is.'

Miss Wise lifted up
Danny's bag.
Danny's face was getting red.
Miss Wise smiled at him.
'I bet you've brought
your favourite toy
to school,' she said.
'Am I right?'

'No! No!' said Danny.

'It's Susie's.'

Miss Wise lifted out
the tools.

'Susie likes **tools**?'
laughed Conor Daly.
'Of course she does,'
said Miss Wise.

'And what else have you
brought, Danny?'
said Miss Wise.
'What's **your own**
favourite toy?'

She reached into
the bag again.

Danny could not say anything.

His face was getting very red.

Miss Wise lifted out

BABY DO IT ALL.

'Danny likes stupid dolls!'
said Conor Daly.

'Conor!' said Miss Wise.
'There's nothing wrong
with liking dolls.
Danny is very good to bring
something for our table.
We can all write about it.'

Oh no! thought Danny.

The teacher handed the doll
to Danny.
'Find a place for it
on the table, Danny,'
she said kindly.

Danny threw **BABY DO IT ALL**
on the table.
'Hee! Hee! Hee!'
said **BABY DO IT ALL**.

'Ho! Ho! Ho!'
laughed Conor Daly.

'What a clever doll!'
said Miss Wise.
'Let's all write a story
about it.'

Danny took out his
writing copy.
It was soaking wet.
Oh no! he thought.

Conor Daly laughed again.
'Teacher! Danny's doll
can wet too!
He should put
a nappy on it.'

Conor Daly
laughed so much
he fell out of his seat.

The other children were
all laughing too.

But Danny wasn't laughing.

He could see **BABY DO IT ALL**
staring at him
from the display table.
He could feel his wet copy
in his hand.

He wanted to run away
and **hide**.

I'll never do anything like this
again, he thought.
Never. Never. Never!

But I think he will, don't you?
Danny's just that kind of kid.